Picture Frames
and other stories

THE WRITIVISM ANTHOLOGY
2013

THE WRITIVISM ANTHOLOGY 2013

E-book and UK/International editions published by
KUSHINDA ISBN 9780957142039

This Africa/Uganda edition published by **Boda Books** ISBN
9789970921706

© Centre For African Cultural Excellence (CACE) and
individual authors

Cover design by Rukundo Joshua

CONTENTS

SHORT-LISTED STORIES

PICTURE FRAMES
Anthea Paelo

The picture frame stood empty on the bedside. Rose had been staring at it for the last half hour, tears running down her face. She held a picture of her husband. He was a big man: tall, fat and strong. The thick glasses he wore barely concealed his bushy eyebrows. The lady seated next to him carried a child. She was much smaller than the man beside her. Her features were delicate and she wore her hair combed out in an afro. The cameraman had caught the slight smile on her face as she gazed at the baby.

Rose straightened out the picture gently, smoothing out the lines, ignoring the tears that dropped on it. Her hair was now styled into a *Janet* haircut, the sides trimmed to allow the hair at the top to stand out. But she was still small. It was that size that had made giving birth to Okello so difficult, and that had made sure he would never have a brother or sister.

She had been so happy then. Daudi was the man of her dreams. He was studying to be a lawyer and had a big future ahead of him. He was also quiet. He seemed almost shy, but when he looked at Rose he made her old worn-out, home-made dress feel like a silk gown. He would show up right after school to carry her books and walk her home. Rose supposed that was the reason she had ignored everything else: his quick temper and the dark moods. No one could be perfect.

Her wedding, when it came, was small. He was still studying and Rose preferred it that way. She was marrying Daudi. That was all that mattered. It had been the happiest day of her life. She did not think she would fall in love with another man, but that had changed when she first looked into her son's face. He was a dark baby with a scrunched up face and healthy lungs. She had never seen a more beautiful sight.

Shaking her head she impatiently wiped her tears with the back of her hand, put the picture in her bag then set it on the suitcase behind her. She turned around, looking at the room, as if to memorise the details. Her eyes lingered on the crib. It had been fifteen years since it had last been used but Rose had found it difficult to give it away. The wardrobe stood on the left side of the bed, one side of it holding empty hangers. Right next to the

1

wardrobe was a sewing machine. She started towards it and then stopped, looking back at the bags behind her, a forlorn expression filling her face. She had sat at that machine and made most of Okello's clothes, sometimes even repairing the tears when they wore thin. It stood stationary, a bright piece of *kitenge* material strewn over it, as if stuck in time, where Rose had been making Okello a shirt two months ago. She glanced at her wristwatch and sat down, a sigh leaving her lips. The cab would soon be here.

*

Breakfast that morning had been a sombre affair – silent, except for the clink of cutlery on plates and the rustle of the newspaper as Daudi read. It had been that way for the last month or so. Rose kept catching herself listening for Okello's footsteps, as if he was just late joining them at the table. It was while she was listening to the silence that she realised Daudi was speaking to her.

"Sorry," her voice came out hoarse; she coughed and tried again, "sorry, what did you say?"

"I said you've swam in pity long enough. It's time you let go." Pushing his nearly empty plate of *katogo* aside, Daudi stood up and put on his coat.

"Pack up his things and put them in the garage. I'll take them to church on Sunday. It's like we are living with his ghost." He shuddered, as if he could sense the ghost there and then.

Rose's heart began to beat so loud that she thought Daudi might hear it.

"His things?"

"Yes, the boy's. Everything." He turned away from her, picking up his laptop bag.

Trembling slightly, Rose stood and whispered, "Okello."

"Hm?" He was stuffing papers on one side of the bag.

Louder, she said, "His name is Okello. Our son's name is Okello."

Daudi turned and Rose did not miss the surprise on his face.

"Rose, you read the letter. You know what he was. It's why he killed himself."

Daudi had always been aloof. Rose had known that when she married him but now he was cold and distant. She had thought that all he needed was a wife to give him a home. After that she had thought that perhaps a child would warm his heart. When he still remained unchanged, she had consoled herself with the fact that he provided for everything she needed. She had been studying to be a tailor when they had met but she had never had to work after they married. Daudi had in fact insisted. But that was okay, she had got Okello soon after. So what if it had happened when he had got drunk and left her with bruises? He had given her a son. Besides, it did not happen often and he was always sorry afterwards. It was the closest he got to warm. And if he spent more days away than at home, he always came back. But this, her child, she could not let him take from her.

"He was a homosexual. We are better off without him." He said the word the way one would refer to a deadly disease, with dread and disgust.

"Remove his things," he continued in a voice that brooked no response, snatching up his keys and stalking away.

Rose slid back onto her chair, deflating like a punctured tyre. For the first time she realised, and accepted, that Daudi would always be Daudi. She would never be free with him. She could not even grieve for her son. Okello had not been perfect and she did not understand this gay business but he was their son.

Rose would remove all his things, but she would go with them.

*

Hearing a car outside, Rose got up from the bed. It was probably the taxi. Walking toward the sewing machine, she picked up the half-made shirt and held it to her chest for a moment, then slowly folded it. She put it in the crib and wiped the dust from the machine. She was going to begin anew, first by making herself a dress. It had been a while since she had last done that. Then maybe she could make dresses for other people, even open that shop she had always dreamed of having. Maybe, somehow, she would find herself again.

THE SIDE WALK
Nassanga Rashidah Sarah

It had begun that morning when the albino Kima got up from what had been her bed for a year. The sun was already peeping out from behind clouds and over the top of a two-storied building. That was her cue, she was late already.

"Timmy! We need to go!"

She gently shook awake her little brother as she cleared the effects of the night off her own face. She then folded their packing crate cardboard bed and stashed it unobtrusively under the wooden steps leading to a phone shop, under which they had slept for two weeks now. Timmy was up already. Kima smoothed down her tattered dress.

"Let's go," she said.

In just two steps, with Timmy clinging onto her arm, they were on the sidewalk and joining the brisk early morning pedestrians.

She helped Timmy along to their work station, which was at the side of the entrance to the City Mall. She sat down cross-legged a few feet in front of him and went to work immediately, stretching out her hands and folding her palms into a seeking bowl. Some passers-by dropped coins into her palms which she would pass on to Timmy for safe keeping. Timmy, who was only five, was of dark complexion and had chubby cheeks, a large nose and big eyes. Their mother had told her that his head had always tilted to the side and that he drooled constantly from birth. Although his brain could not align all his actions, there were two things he never forgot - that Kima was all he had and that the moneybag was to be guarded with his life.

Their parents had been lynched two years before, in their village of Tamu, on the orders of the witchdoctor. In a backwater village of perfectly black people, two children with rare health conditions equalled sorcery. One day the headman's son had discovered a human skull in their house. Kima had been just six years old the day her parents died in front of her, the miracle was that the villagers were too scared of her and Timmy to kill them too.

With no relatives to take them in, the devil's children

4

walked to the city, forty kilometres away. Kima was a beautiful eight year old girl with her albino complexion, squinty eyes and curly brown hair. People gave her alms for the sake of her frailty, she looked as if she were about to die. It was this success that put her on a collision course with Mamadou and her twins.

They arrived at 10 a.m. As usual Mamadou, a middle-aged, dark woman in perfect health, who deliberately wore torn clothes, dropped the twins off before heading to her own station just across the road. The only thing that differentiated the twins was a mole on one of their cheeks.

"She's early again! We have to get rid of her!" One of them said to the other.

They stared at Kima scornfully and spat each time she got a coin, or a note, when they didn't.

Mamadou watched and compared the four children's begging skills from her station across the street. A fat woman, with extraordinary breasts and obviously no bra, dropped a coin in Kima's hand, who gave it to her accursed brother. Mamadou hated them, for they were sapping the spirit of her own children, dampening their enthusiasm for their work. Well, she would do something to sort them out permanently.

At around midday a short, dark man, with a tick in his right eye, came to a halt a meter from where Kima was seated. He pulled out a twenty from his wallet and handed it to her. She couldn't believe her eyes! All day she had received only coins and a single one thousand shilling note, but not a twenty, not in weeks. Kima was near speechless but she forced out the words.

"Thank you so much, uncle! Thank you!"

She looked at him teary eyed, albeit grinning. Apollo grunted and went on his way without a second look at her. She shrugged, she had a fortune in hand and her stomach demanded more attention than his behaviour. They had enough to get them something to eat. The money in the bag, which Timmy guarded with his life, would be for his medicine. Kima had it all planned out.

She jogged to a nearby kiosk. The attendant looked down at her as if she was a piece of trash, but she didn't stop smiling.

Besides, most people gave her that indecent look, it no longer hurt her feelings as it used to.

"What do you want?" he snapped. "There are no free things here. Go back to the streets where you belong!"

She held out the twenty and spoke breathlessly. "Give me three chapattis, two…"

"What is this?" he interrupted. "You think I'm stupid? This note is a fake!" He spat at her in the sudden outrage of a petty shopkeeper. "Today, you'll learn a lesson!"

He grabbed her arm. Kima could feel his fang-like fingers digging into her flesh. She let out a loud cry.

"It was just given to me!" Whatever *it* was, it was time to plead and she knew it.

"Just shut up," he shouted, several times, as he dragged her to the nearby police post.

Behind the counter stood a massive woman in police uniform; her round face had wrinkles across the forehead, with huge nostrils and red eyes that scared Kima to shivers. Her gaze was steadily fixed on the shopkeeper who was busy exaggerating the incident. Whenever Kima tried to interrupt she was shut up by a fierce look, it was clear the policewoman would believe the shopkeeper. Kima was a *nobody*, she was terrified for her Timmy but she was filth and not worth the benefit of the doubt. The policewoman scribbled down a few things and signalled to a tired looking police guard, who was sitting on a wooden bench behind her, to take Kima away. She tried to resist but that earned her a slap on the cheek, her eyes tearing up immediately.

They stopped at a metallic, burglar proofed door where the police guard pulled out a bunch of keys from his pocket.

"Silly kids, I don't know why they run away from their homes to the streets! Wasting our time when we have bigger criminals to catch."

He thrust her into the small room so that she landed flat on the cold concrete floor. The room smelled of piss and fear. Tears welled up in her eyes once more as she wondered what would befall helpless Timmy, for she knew she wasn't going to get out any time soon. The world Timmy knew would have ended for him when she was marched away.

Apollo flicked the one thousand shilling notes with his thumb and first finger, the tick in his eye keeping faster time than ever as he counted. "This money is less than it should be by one thousand shillings," he declared.

"Meaning what, huh? We agreed on five thousand shillings and it is all there," replied Mamadou.

Apollo's response was to grab the shawl around her neck and pull it tight to strangle her. Mamadou did not need anyone to tell her to start screaming. Her six year old boys looked on, helpless, lost. A crowd quickly gathered and a brave man with rippling muscles pulled Apollo away from certain murder.

Still huffing and puffing, Apollo shouted, "You bitch! Your little bitch rival is in the slammer for good. You pay me the six thousand shillings, or else…"

TOGETHER
Kathryn Kazibwe

Mixed feelings whirl around within me as I step into my sister's living room. I am swamped by nostalgia so potent that I can almost hear the laughter.

My sister is nestled in the red leather loveseat to my right, humming to a fat baby in her arms. The receding rays of the sun, from the French window behind her, form a soft halo. It is a scene of perfection, a mother looking down at her own spitting image, just like me and my Zawadi. I clutch the lapels of my jacket tightly to my chest. I feel my heart beating frantically and I take a few deep breaths, it will not do to cry before I even say a word.

"Naluyange," I say.

She looks up at me. The humming stops. Her face is expressionless, her eyes vacant. For a moment I imagine she doesn't recognize me. I nibble on my lower lip.

"Nakyeyune?"

"Hello," I say. What a flat word to say to my own sister, whom I have not seen for the better part of two years. My mind casts around for the words I had prepared to say. Nothing. I search Naluyange's face, but apart from the set of her lips she lets nothing on.

She leans forward and, with shaking hands, places the baby in a bassinet at the foot of her chair. He promptly sticks his little fist in his mouth and sucks ardently. When she looks back up at me, my sister's face is a collage of emotions.

"So you finally show up," she says. I can tell she is trying hard not to shout.

She watches as I walk towards her and settle next to her. She smells of breast milk and Johnson's baby powder, with her trademark *Victoria's Secret* perfume pushing through. I want to hug her, to take everything back to the way it used to be, but I am afraid. I consider reaching for her hand but the look on her face stops me short. I crack my knuckles.

"I'm really sorry, Naluyange," I say, looking into her eyes.

"Sorry? For what? Be specific, because there's quite a bit you need to apologise for."

I turn away. I deserve that. Her voice is heavy with her

challenge to me to admit my misdeeds, to explain why I have estranged myself from my baby sister - my best friend and only remaining family - for so long. I have almost convinced myself it was with good reason, but at the back of my mind Maama's voice won't let me rest. I could have come sooner.

I clear my throat.

"It hasn't been easy, Naluyange."

"That's no excuse! It hasn't been easy for any of us!"

"I know, but..."

"No, you don't. You know nothing, Nakyeyune! Maama asked for you. Every day, till the end." Naluyange shakes her head with emphasis on each word. "Do you know how that felt, Nakyeyune? Telling her you would come yet I couldn't reach you?"

I try to imagine it. Our mother, calling for me from her deathbed. I cannot.

"Well, I know what it felt like to be on the receiving end of her spite all my life. I was never good enough for her, you know that," I say.

"For Christ's sake, she was dying! You owed her an audience, at the very least," she says, flailing her arms about and almost hitting my face.

"You would never understand. You always were the *good* one." The sharp tone in my voice catches me by surprise. I look down at my hands, willing them to unclench from the fists they have formed.

In the silence that follows my sister folds the sides of her green kitenge onto her lap, revealing a gap of red leather between us.

This is not how I envisioned this discussion.

"You could have at least come for the burial," she finally says.

"Look Naluyange, Maama hated my guts. I've made my peace with that and I'm not here to have that argument with you."

She nods.

"So why are you here, anyway? You wouldn't bury Maama, not even visit to meet your nephew, so what is it?" She turns to face me. Our knees almost touch.

I fight the tightness in my throat; the doubts, the shame, the guilt. Her raised eyebrows don't do much to boost my confidence.

"I'm here because I need your help. I..."

Naluyange frowns as she cuts me off, a raised hand in my face.

"You need help? You know, Nakyeyune, you can't just waltz in here after marooning yourself, Lord knows where, and expect me to fall over myself for you! I barely know you now!"

"I barely know myself either," I murmur.

I turn my eyes to the painting on the opposite wall, of women with babies on their backs and baskets on their heads. They stand so straight, like they cannot feel the weight.

It hits me again how selfish it is for me to be here, seeking solace from the very person I have been actively pushing away. Yet I remain with no options. I think of the endless nights I have spent crying, dreading the nightmares; mangled bodies, pointing fingers, keening cries.

"Zawadi died."

The words fall like an anvil, the deafening clang reverberating in my mind. I hear Naluyange's sharp intake of breath. I keep my eyes on the women in the painting. I watch them blur, their toothy smiles warping through my tears.

"What?"

My sister lifts my clasped hands from my lap and cradles them in hers. I want to tell her I am fine, that I have had a while to mourn, that she should save the tears I can hear welling in her voice. But the lump in my throat will not allow me to.

"Why... Why didn't you say something? You just... Oh my God, Sis! Did you bury him alone?"

It is the way she says "*Sis*". Tears begin to flow down my cheeks.

"I slept as my baby died," I whisper. I look through my tears at the blurry shape that is my sister. "I killed my Zawadi!"

Naluyange leans forward and hugs me. It has been so long, but my body remembers this embrace. I hold on tight as the tears fight to drain from my eyes. I sob until I am afraid my throat might tear, spilling gravel all over her chest.

"Tell me what happened."

I take a deep breath and recount the details of the day my life was turned on its head. I stare at my nephew, now asleep, a little smile touching his rosy lips.

He looks so much like my Zawadi, the day I found him in his cot. Peaceful. But on that dawn my baby's eyelids did not flutter. His chest did not rise and fall. I couldn't wake him. I screamed his name - screamed and screamed - but he did not wake up.

"Good mothers don't let their babies die," I sob. I ache inside because I know I will never be better than Maama always said. "I should have checked on him earlier, should have known he needed me. I should have *done* something!"

"Shhh, shhh, no," Naluyange says. "It's alright. You will be fine."

"Will I? I don't know if I can go through this."

Naluyange repeatedly pats my braided hair until her kitenge is soaked through and the tears have ebbed to sniffles.

"I'm here for you. I've always been. We will do it together."

THE SHADOW
Emmeline Bisiikwa

"How could you, Danny?" I felt a lump rise to my throat, choking me. "Tell me, what has she got that I haven't? Is she more of a woman? Prettier?"

He paced the floor of the living room in that annoying way, walking back and forth in three swift steps, one-two-three, one-two-three, as if he could not stay still in a place for long or wanted to be in another place. His brows were creased in a frown.

"Damn it, talk to me Danny!"

"Calm down woman!" He stopped pacing. "You're going to wake the children." He walked off into the connecting room.

I dug my fingers into the sides of the tiger print love seat, trying to ease my breathing. Betrayal was a bitter syrup especially when served by the one you loved. When he returned with his car keys and headed for the door I impulsively ran to it and blocked his exit. "You expect me to take this lying down? We built a life together. You can't throw it away for some other bitch!"

"Stop!" His eyes came aflame with anger. "Do not call her that. She is ten times the woman you will ever be!"

I felt anger begin to bubble in my chest. How could he shamelessly defend her? I longed to smash something heavy on his head, anything, to make him hurt as much as I did. Instead, I simply stood there as his nose flared in anger and his chest heaved. He pushed me aside and strode out, slamming the door with a force that rattled the hinges.

It had all started early that morning. Cecile, my best friend, called me at the ungodly hour of 4am. "Have you watched the news, Jess?" She was wheezing, as if she had returned from a marathon.

"Did you happen to check the time, Cecile? It's only..."

'Put on NTV!'

I dropped the phone, jumped out of bed and switched on the TV. When the pictures danced before my eyes I staggered and fell onto the bed. My vision blurred for a moment. I ran to his bedroom, pushed through his door and switched on the fluorescent light. He lay in bed, sleeping, legs curled up like our firstborn Jamie's, hands pillowing his head. Perhaps it was all some sort of joke.

He turned on his side as the light shone on his face and soon opened his eyes. "What are you doing here?" He asked, a hand blocking the glare of the light.

"I saw it on the news."

He began to sit up. "What are you talking about?"

"You and... a lady."

He dropped his hand and began to sit up. I grabbed his wallet that lay on his table and flipped it open. He came at me and grabbed me by the shoulders trying to snatch it away. A picture slipped out and glided to the floor. He stopped then as I picked it up. My hands shook. He stood there watching as I trembled. I stared at the picture of him and the same beautiful woman from the TV. Then he snatched it from my hands with an abruptness that startled me. He set it back in his wallet. "How dare you?" I cried. He did not even try to defend himself, but walked out of the room.

And so, when he said "She is ten times the woman you will ever be!" I knew he was lost to me. He went on to move in with Alicia that very day.

Later that day, my mother called and her breezy voice asked "Are you okay child?" I burst into tears. I sat there, the phone by my ear, as mother's voice went from caring to concern. "He left me, Mother. He left!" She cooed and muttered sounds that were supposed to make me feel better. It used to work when I was younger.

"How am I supposed to go on without him, Mother?"

"You lived before him Jess. Just go take a shower, you will feel better, and get the girls over to my place now."

After I had returned from taking Jamie and Hari to Mother's place, Danny's mother came. She walked in stiffly, refused to acknowledge my greeting, but instead asked that I move out of her son's house along with my daughters. She said he was marrying another woman who would give him a son. She wore a superior smile, as if she was someone I would never be.

"Is that why you always disliked me? You wanted a grandson?"

"I don't dislike you, I just knew my Daniel could do better."

My head spun as I fought the urge to shake her shoulders until she was quivering.

"I gave him everything!"

"You gave him nothing."

"He is everything to me!"

"Maybe that's the problem, Jess. You haven't had a life, so when he asked you to marry him you jumped at the idea. Was it the money?"

"I love him! Danny is the love of my life!" My vision was blurred by tears. "Don't tear us apart!"

She laughed. "Surely you must have had a contingency plan? How could you have failed to see this coming Jessica?"

"Please leave."

"You are sending me away, young woman? From my son's house?"

"Leave now!"

She wore a satisfied smile on her face when she opened the door, "I do not want you here by tomorrow."

I sank onto the sofa. Our pictures hung on the wall. On one side was the gold framed picture of Danny and I on our wedding day, smiling as if the world was our own paradise. On the other side of the wall were pictures of our two lovely daughters, Jamie and Hari, one for every birthday. I looked at the bit of paint that was freshly scrubbed from when Hari drew on it with her crayons. I wondered how they would feel when they found out that their father had chosen a woman over them. Jamie had never slept a night without Danny tucking her into bed, and when he wasn't in town he always called to bid her goodnight. Hari wouldn't worry much, I knew, because she fancied herself my 'handbag'.

Danny.

I had become his shadow and as I sat on that sofa I finally understood what drives people to suicide. There, enveloped by the pictures of what used to be and what still is, I felt it - bubbles of anger, then hopelessness. I got up and began to pack Jamie's, Hari's and my belongings. After I had heaped our luggage into the SUV I returned to the house that had been my marital home. I lit a match and held it to the hem of the curtain that ran from corner to corner of the sitting room wall.

In the rear view mirror, as I sped away, I saw the faint hint of smoke wafting from the windows like a shadow - melting, floating and merging with the gloomy cloud above, chasing me, becoming me. I felt it then, a surge of emotion so great it had my stomach heaving and my knees wobbling. I held fast onto the steering wheel as the car veered off the tarmac, but I regained control and swung back onto the road. I breathed in deeply, tasting my own tears as they dripped into my mouth.

Then, I waited for his call.

EMOTIONAL ROLLER COASTER
Paul Kisakye

A loud knock on the door startled me. With frenzied keystrokes, I typed out a reply to my boyfriend, Joel. "Get back to you. Someone's at the door."

I logged out of Facebook.

While getting my legs into a pair of shorts, I heard the knock again, this time louder. Did someone want to break down my door?

I opened the door and beamed. "Sanyu!"

My best friend was standing in front of me. The smile on my face disappeared when I saw that she was on the verge of tears.

"Just hold me, David," Sanyu said, her shoulders slumped and her eyes downcast.

I pulled her to myself and hugged her. I pushed my hostel room door closed with my left hand.

Sanyu's shoulders shook with heavy sobs. I held her tighter.

"It's Jimmy, isn't it?" I asked, almost in a whisper.

Sanyu nodded.

"Hush." I stroked her back. "There. There."

When the hug turned awkward, I moved a step back and wiped the tears from her eyes with my thumbs.

"Can I get you a drink?" I asked, clearing my throat.

"That would be nice," Sanyu said. She sat on the bed.

I had turned a corner of my room into a kitchenette. It had a table on which I'd stacked a few melamine plates and tumblers which I used to eat takeout food with my friends, especially when I didn't want to spend on disposable crockery. Apart from the plates, there was a bottle of Uganda Waragi and a large, plastic bottle of Coke. I poured two glasses of Waragi and offered one to Sanyu.

"So, tell me," I said, sitting on the bed next to her, "what did Jimmy do this time?"

"I'm not going back," Sanyu said. "I have had enough of his games. He treats me like trash. He beats me. See for yourself." She unzipped her jacket and pulled the blouse up to show bruises on her belly. "There's more on my back."

A string of obscenities escaped my lips. This was not the first time Sanyu had told me about Jimmy's unfaithfulness but I had

16

not imagined that Jimmy could stoop so low as to raise his hand and hit a girl. I had advised her over and over again to leave him. *That guy is lucky that I have not met him yet,* I thought. *Otherwise his neck would have had a dislocated bone by now.*

"But I love him."

"You are putting your love where it doesn't belong, baby," I said.

Sanyu's voice raised an octave higher and she fought hard to keep her emotions in check. "How can he repay me like this for my love? I've never hurt him, David. I've never hurt him." A wave of sobs rocked her small body.

"Cry it out, baby," I said. "Cry it out lest you break."

Thus encouraged, Sanyu cried, and cried, and cried some more. I kept speaking soothingly in her ears while caressing her back.

When her crying turned into whimpering and finally stopped, I let her go, stood up from the bed and looked down at her. "So are you going to take that drink or not? I still have half a bottle there." I pointed in the direction of my kitchenette.

Sanyu contorted her face into a mischievous grin, tilted her head and poured the contents of her tumbler down her throat.

"That's my girl!" I said, smiling.

I picked up the bottle of Waragi, opened it and refilled her tumbler.

"Thanks," Sanyu said. She lifted her tumbler like she was proposing a toast.

"All guys are jerks," I said. "Don't let them screw you. You deserve a good life."

Sanyu nodded her head and said, "To a good life." Then she raised her tumbler again.

I raised my tumbler too. "To the best life you've ever dreamed of, free of Jimmy."

And we both burst out into uncontrollable laughter.

"Let's party," Sanyu said. "Put on some music." She then worked up my laptop and within a minute Maurice Kirya's voice wafted from my subwoofer.

Sanyu downed her Waragi, stood up and started dancing. I joined her, my strokes a little uncoordinated, which got us laughing all over again.

As Maurice Kirya's *Malaika* started playing, she held my hand and drew me towards her. I wrapped my arms around her and we swayed to the smooth ballad. We continued dancing to four or five other songs until Sanyu asked me a question that caused my heart to stop beating.

"Why can't you be straight, just for me?"

My whole body stiffened.

"I know you love Joel and all that, but you're the best guy I've ever met."

"What?"

"You know what I mean, David." Sanyu extricated herself from my arms and pushed me onto the bed.

"I think you're drunk," I said, my eyes as wide as saucers.

"You bet I am. And very, very horny."

Sanyu shrugged her jacket off and started unbuttoning her blouse. "Don't!" I said, trying to move my limbs so I could stop her but failing.

She got her blouse off, crawled onto the bed and got on top of me. Her lips brushed mine. I closed my eyes and kissed her back, tasting alcohol on her tongue.

I felt her hand grab my crotch and I let out a moan. Her fingers fumbled with the fly of my shorts and pulled down the zip.

"Ohmygod! You have no underwear on?"

I awoke with a start!

I was naked. I was not alone in bed. And the person on the other side of the bed was not Joel. It was a girl. A stunningly beautiful girl with lips slightly curved in a dreamy smile.

Sanyu. It was Sanyu.

The events of last night flooded my memory with staggering clarity.

I picked up my phone from the bedside table, right next to the empty Waragi bottle. I had nine new messages from Joel.

LONG-LISTED STORIES

BUTTERFLIES COME AT DAWN
Solomon Manzi

The rain fell rhythmically, beating out a musical clatter upon the tin roof.

As if in unspoken concordance, the woman's belly rose and fell in slight motions. Slight, yet the child's eyes followed the ebbs intently, like a feline in the dark.

Then suddenly, as if in a deliberate attempt to break the rhythm, the woman coughed once and rolled over in the clumsy way that is characteristic of sleeping bodies.

The child stared on, as if in a trance, her delicate ears twitching with the sounds of the falling rain; capturing the silent explosions of the water-globes as they struck the red earth, dislodging dust specks by their millions.

The child sneezed; the sneeze of a tiny lump of fragility, her light frame shuddering with the shock of it. Her name was Kagezi, and she was ten.

The falling rain was now a uniform wall of sound and, as her eyelids became heavier, a tiny smile tickled the child's lips. She let it spread.

Over the past year Kagezi had grown close to two feet tall. She now stood a few inches below the rusty iron bolt on the inside of the front door, a feat she had never imagined manageable when she was a tiny dwarf only twelve months back.

And the fact that she was nearly ten years old now, didn't help matters either. She still was much smaller than all the girls her age around the village.

'The little dwarf of Nyamiyaga!' her peers often teased her.

Even at Nyakyojo Preparatory school, where she was in her Standard six, Kagezi never fared any better.

Teachers always picked on her to respond, when the rest of the class was silent on subjects that were clearly beyond children their age. Why in the world would they consider her knowledgeable on riddles like 'Photosynthesis?'

She may have appeared diminutive, but Kagezi was definitely not small on big headedness.

Once, on an early and cold morning four years ago, when she had still lived with her grandmother in rural Kisoro, Kagezi had stood atop a termite mound near the edge of a cliff overlooking a densely forested ravine, just a few meters from the house.

Now, this was no ordinary ravine, for it fell sharply on both sides before halting its descent to assume an awkward gentleness of slope. As if intent on further eluding normality the ravine bore in its middle a river of fast-flowing waters, which sinuously wound its way across the valley, hidden from aerial view under a thick canopy of trees, brambles and bushes.

On that day however, upon the termite mound, in the same spot she had risen and ran to every morning since she was three, Kagezi had held her breath and stretched forth her tiny palms, fingers sticking out, attempting to give the yet visible half of the sun a spiky- hair look.

The little girl had closed her eyes.

She had listened to the wind, as it blew in an invisible mass across the great valley, stirring up life in its journey – the singing of the birds, the quivering of the leaves, the distant chatters of monkeys – she had felt it all, and she had felt little no more.

Her mind saw outstretched limbs – the limbs of a giant, not of a diminutive ten year old. She felt that she could bound across the great green rift in a single skip, or leap and hug the fluffy clouds that were captivatingly gilded by the sun's bright rays, if she pleased.

She could be tall and mighty, Kagezi!

She would dare!

But, on this night, Kagezi snuggled-on behind her unseen protective hedge.

Drifting deeper into sleep, her ears danced to strange tunes as they picked up the gurgles of small streams being born on the outside; and as the streamlets sprouted, she could hear, distantly, the responsive frolics of pebbles and small rocks as they rolled about in the wetting soil.

All night, the mother of the growing streams persisted in her earthward journey, like an implacable mistress unrepentant in her resolve to quench the lusts and thirsts of a waiting earth, who responded with an almost commensurate fervour in impassioned absorption of his mistress' loving.

*

"Kagezi *Wee!*" the shrill voice punctured her hedge like a gleaming sword.

In her world of dreams, Kagezi could see the rays play like mice along its glistening edges.

She smiled delightedly, revealing her dark gums where the milk teeth had fallen out.

Now, the mice were sprouting wings and fluttering like multi-coloured butterflies before her eyes, sending her delight racing paces higher.

The woman lumbered into the room then, to establish the reason for her daughter's passivity, a stingy scold poised at the tip of her tongue.

Clearly, Munema was a heavy set woman of light complexion, whose jovial personality and dimpled cheeks were charms which Mondo, Kagezi's late father, had found irresistible years before, when she had inarguably been the most adorable maiden in Busanza.

Of course, Munema had not been so heavy set then, or for that matter, heavy set at all.

Her face had not been creased, and neither did her eyes harbour a permanent blankness, resultant from years of crying over her husband's brutal murder one night as he returned from a late party.

She had sobbed for months after the tragedy, and nearly seven years later the shadows of rueful nostalgia still haunted her big, dark eyes.

This morning however, Munema found her daughter snoring lightly, muffled giggles shaking the girl's tiny body.

The woman shook her head knowingly, the scold instinctively abandoning its perch upon her tongue.

"Kagezi, the chickens must be fed, do wake up..." The woman's voice was now barely distinguishable from the chirpings of the brightly plumaged birds that had replaced the fluttering butterflies, in the child's dream, as a firm but gentle hand rocked her.

Kagezi awoke with a grumble and, as her eyes opened, couldn't help squinting with displeasure. Her tiny pair of hands clasped her mother's rocking hand tightly.

The brightening morning bore a very sharp contrast to the

benign luminescence of Kagezi's dream.

"I love you so much Mommy!" The declaration shocked Munema pleasantly as the child sat up slowly, disarming her mother further with her tenderly infectious smile.

The woman swept the girl up from the rumpled layers of bedding, drawing her bosom-ward in the habitual manner of African women overcome with motherly sentiment. The minutes, in an apparent connivance, appeared to slow from their usual trot to a near stroll, permitting the ethereal display of love to come alive with a fierce intensity.

Mother and child winced with a painful pleasure, the reciprocal grip tightening in a mutual effort to galvanise their oneness. It was as if they dared say to a world that would inevitably attempt to sever their union, that theirs was inseparable.

"Come now my angel, my lovely and strong woman, Kikaazi..." whispered the mother, gently stroking the dark curls on the child's head in the way that only mothers can. Kagezi raised her face from its warm haven on her mother's shoulder and, with typical eclecticism, shone her beguiling eyes at Munema's face, quipping "I am hungry, Mommy!"

The woman's heart skipped. She smiled.

"Please let me feed the chickens after my porridge ... you made porridge this morning, didn't you?" importuned the girl.

A strange light began to dance in the woman's eyes. She swept her gaze across the tiny face, as if in search of some concealed mischief, and was torn between scolding and laughter.

Munema struggled to resist the playful smile that was, in all un-timeliness, beginning to provoke the linings of her lips.

Unconsciously, Munema squeezed her daughter tighter, causing the girl to yelp like a petrified puppy before loosening the clasp.

And, as she released the child, the woman swore.

"Why, you little elf! Tricking poor me, Munema, daughter of Hillaria! But, hmmm, children of these days..."

A rocking laughter got the better of her and, arms akimbo, the woman's firm bosom heaved with an intense delight that could only have echoed from her inmost soul.

"Eish, Kagezi! I should have known you were up to one of

your *Bu-geziis* again!" lamented Munema, employing her coined term for the child's innumerable shenanigans.

This time, both broke out laughing, Kagezi beginning to feel slightly awkward at her mother's atypical off-handedness.

"God bless my ageing soul…"supplicated the woman, inquiring of the girl, "how, by the way, were you able to tell that it was porridge for breakfast today, I thought you were deep asleep all along?"

Kagezi raised her left hand, small and delicate, to her quivering lips and yawned before retorting coyly "but mommy, it was all in my dream, they come true you know!"

The girl dashed through the open door.

"Kagezi! Kagezi *wee*!" was all Munema could yell in her futile entreaties to summon the elf, whose tiny feet were carrying her swiftly towards the chicken house to do Mommy's bidding.

THE NEW POLITICIAN
Angella Sandra Namwase

Your fingers are tucked into the mini pockets of your grey striped dress, your "Sunday best" as you call it, it is all you have to wear that you think suitable for a Campaign such as this. You take short, restless strides. You are shaking off the memory of Chuma.

You steal a look at Ruth over your shoulder and the sight of her makes you even more impatient. You want to be like her. You want to walk like her, look like her, have loads of money like her. Only that you don't dream of spending your money paying tuition for poor people like she does, the changes you want to make are bigger than that. Her friends, who attempt to dress like her, hold a big white umbrella above her head whenever she steps outside, like hired bodyguards. The umbrella's golden handle makes you feel you could be purchased by it alone... if, that is, you were still "for sale". Her slim bodice curves up to the chest like those sculptures made in *Akamba Village*, the African crafts territory you wish you might own someday. Her behind pushes against her short grey dress; unlike yours, it looks like one of those dresses from the catwalk of Sylvia Owori, the famous designer whose creations grace every fashion billboard in Kampala.

"Chuma, I'm..." you had bitten your lip as the tears rolled down your cheeks, "I am done with this. I am so done with this."

"What? What do you mean ' you're done'?"

"Exactly that. I am done."

"Oh, so you finally figured it out," he had grabbed your arm, "so you have found someone more loaded, a fancy new pimp, or what?"

"That's not your business. I am through with this."

The first year boys, who call themselves "guys", pass by with their eyes fixed on her, like dogs salivating over roasted meat, and say, "Ruth is so pretty, let's go and vote for her." Your ears are open wide enough not to miss this and your heart begins to gallop.

You step up to the platform.

"What this association needs is an empowered woman, one who will put women's rights as her utmost priority..."

As you begin your speech your sunken eyes roll towards a wooden table in the furthest corner of the room; clothes, shoes and dirty dishes are strewn across it, unattended. You are hungry. Your eye catches a big coloured poster you wish you didn't have to see, the woman on the poster looks like those milky, smooth-faced women from western Uganda. Below her are the words *Vote Ruth Kitaka for Women Affairs Secretary.* You struggle to ignore it and go on, "I hope, however, to serve for the benefit of everyone in this university..."

"Gal," (he sounds like Chuma, this man in the crowd, he utters the word as though he's rehearsing it, "*Hello, gal, how are you doin' gal?*" Chuma would say) "Gal, we shall give you our vote," the man in the crowd shouts, "We are convinced gal, you are 'real', we shall vote for you."

You look at him and see the memories in his eyes. He and the other two, now standing like staring sculptures in the corner of the room, had once grabbed you on Lumumba Street, where your one inch skirt had been enough to signal your commercial ambitions. Four hours later they had all pulled up their trousers, gasping like they had been digging in the large Nakasozi gardens. They had fastened their belts with immense satisfaction, as though they rose from answering a call that had been retained in their bowels for a long time. Your eyes had focused on the holes in their trousers dancing on their knees as you waited for the clinking of coins, the sound that would make you forget your daily work and comfort your soul. A sound that could help you survive without Chuma.

"Good luck gal!" the other two men in the room yell at you.

"*Gal, it's been long since you last visited me,*" Chuma would say, whenever he wanted another round, and when he was done he would provide you with more customers. "*Vero, I think you should leave him,*" your friends told you more than once, "*because this will lead to your grave some day. I wonder why you don't think of this pain whenever you're with him.*"

"*I know! But I promise, this is the last time,*" you answered just as often.

But the neighbourhood near your hostel overflows with streams of grey water with black lumps in it, it is filled with the

27

stench of rotting fish-heads and the sight of children splashing about in the grey water; Chuma's big jeans, red sneakers and twisted accent had fed your hunger for a better life.

Earlier, you watched your fellow contestant, Ruth Kitaka, slip dollars into the box of the final year students who preside over the election process. It was your first time to see dollars. You were ashamed to drop your five hundred shilling coin into the box, but the student in charge accepted it and waved you on by.

Now you are standing at the lectern and already you feel victorious.

"Wewe, wewe! Raah-aah-cha!" You shout as you finish.

The audience is stirred into excitement and they cheer back, "Oh yeah!"

You step down. You keep pacing. Your grey dress is wet beneath your armpits.

It's almost the end of voting and your puffy eyes are still focused on the transparent ballot boxes.

Finally, the stout man's voice pierces through your drowsy mind.

"I hereby declare that Veronica Kironde has been elected the Secretary for Women Affairs 2013."

You stand up in astonishment. The noise in the room makes your head pound, bringing tears to your eyes. You are amazed at the equality you now have with Ruth Kitaka, the minister's daughter. You are surprised by the new identity that you have suddenly acquired in society as Veronica Kironde, the "New Politician".

CHOICES IN DANGER
Emmanuel Ssebaggala

From as early as I can remember, I knew I didn't fit the pigeonholes. Dad would take me to play football and I would be desperate to come to the end of it. I loved sitting with the girls to talk about fashion and make-up while the boys played games. It felt natural for me to be around girls. Boys seemed different, the few times I tried to hang out with them I felt out of place and awkward.

When the politics of the playground changed, around puberty, I began to struggle with identity. Girls hung out and talked about boys, and boys hung out and talked about girls. I didn't feel like I fitted in anywhere. I ditched my make-up kit in exchange for football, only to feel more isolated than ever. My waking moments were filled with fantasies of coming out, my nights haunted by nightmares of consequent rejection and suicide. I tried so hard to be like the other boys but I hated every second of it. My anxiety edged me to build my life around the one thing I had control of at the time - my education - and like a faithful servant I was rewarded with unparalleled distinctions throughout. I thought that, with such commendable achievements in my academics, society would be blind to my lack of experience in winning the hearts of members of the opposite team. If they did see it, probably they convinced themselves that it was the price I paid for academic excellence.

In the wake of suicidal thoughts that had sneaked their way back into my racing mind, it became clear to me that I did not really want to die. True, society's comments about those I identified with were fire and brimstone: the *sick people* and the *normal people* lived in a most fragile peace as life seemed to have an unknown expiration date for the *sick, gay people*. I had dated Rachael, and Susan, and Jackie! We fell out when they realized I was competition for male affection, rather than a source. On many of our dates I had described male beauty with tangible lust and I was a disappointment during secluded moments. One morning, after a disappointing evening, in front of the entire class, Rachael had baptised me the "Generation's oldest all-time plump virgin". She had flunked me socially yet saved me a worse label, that of the perverted, promiscuous queer I would have become if she had revealed her confirmations. For that, she was a confidante worth keeping.

With the impeccable recommendations that my academic excellence and moral conduct fetched me, fate dictated that I deserved the Master's Degree Programme I applied for in Europe. Europe seemed similar to Uganda until the starry night of the freshman ball, when a classmate who had made it a pastime of his to keep tabs on my social life, particularly its lack of female company, walked up to me. "Hi, I am Kateregga," his accent was very familiar, "may I have this dance?" Did he know? I knew it was Europe, but how could he be so bold? For God sakes he was Ugandan, he should know better! Our conversations over the next weeks revealed that he had fled the country under similar circumstances.

Our acquaintanceship blossomed into romance.

*

Two days ago, I returned for our first wedding anniversary. Grace's pleas to be devoured like any other married woman were met with echoes of, *"Honey, it was a long flight, I need my rest to recharge."*

Was it the thudding of her palm as it hit my cheek that woke me up? Or was it the pain that followed? Grumbling, I fumbled through the open texts on the phone she slapped in my face. "What is this?" she demanded. Guilty as charged, I could only run so far. I had nothing in common with the man our families had arranged for her to marry.

"I wanted to tell you, but we barely knew each other except that our fathers are best friends since high school. I am gay and Kateregga is my partner. I didn't mean for you to find out this way."

I wished she could say something – anything – to express her thoughts but the room only picked echoes of her breathing. As she disappeared through the lounge and into the study I told myself that she needed to think things through.

*

In the stillness of the night, I was awakened by the buzzing of your phone at the arrival of a new text. "That farewell dinner was rich. I am full and well nourished; I could go for days without craving your juices- Kate." During our honeymoon you talked of sex as if it were food. I flicked on my bedside lamp to scroll through a previous exchange of texts between you and Kate – or so I thought.

Kateregga! You were very close then, even now, but isn't that typical of the groom and his best man? What is it about me that turned you gay? Was it because I could not trade my whole life here for a fresh start with you in Europe? What will people say when they find out I was never enough for my husband and he turned gay? This must be my stepmother reaching out from her grave to mock me.

How can you get caught between the sun and the moon?
They are like a thousand miles apart;
Yet that's where I have crashed.
The audacity with which you described his beauty;
I have never felt so ugly and unworthy of a man's love.
Being on the edge is a dark and lonely feeling,
You've ruined my life;
I am only returning the favour.
I hope our son embraces having a father for a mother.
Happy Anniversary

The guilt of Grace taking her own life ripped my life at the seams. Memories of her cold body lying on the floor of the study, next to an empty tin of tranquilisers, on the morning of our anniversary, with her last piece of writing secured between her hands and her chest, keep haunting me...

31

GRANDPA'S STORY
Muhwezi Simpson

I have been thinking of the story, about a girl, which my grandpa told me.

Once upon a time in Grandpa's village, he had said, there was a young and beautiful girl called Rose. Her beauty attracted men in their hundreds, married and unmarried. They yearned to have her as one of their wives. But she was not ready for marriage. In spite of the fierce competition that emerged among them to win her, she was headstrong and this made it difficult for them. Some men gave up, while others persisted. Most of them, although rich and able to pay any dowry her parents asked, were quite old.

"I will only get married when I feel I'm ready, and to a man who will be capable of loving me properly," Rose said.

One day she woke up early. It was the day long-awaited, on which she was to prove her worth on the pitch. It was the first time she had qualified for the national championship. As she opened the door the cold hit her, almost making her turn back. She washed her face then walked to the store to check if the milk was still full. It was as she had left it the previous night.

She picked a broom and began scratching the dusty ground. Water was also missing from the empty pot. "Let me finish all the work quickly, so that I catch the running competition," the thoughts rang in her mind.

She preferred a big calabash to the smaller, heavier pot and the shortest route to the river was a small trail which traversed the valley. After a few meters she heard an odd sound, coming from behind, of stepping feet. She turned but didn't see anyone; she didn't mind if somebody was there, after all, the path was not hers alone.

She heard whispers. Feeling nervous, she turned. A tall man stood just behind her, others stood behind him. Black mud was smeared all over their bodies, which made Rose tremble with fear. "Run!" her heart prompted. She took a deep breath and took off. The three followed, she knew the chase was on so she threw the calabash on the ground to gather speed.

The race took them to the river in the steep, v-shaped valley where it moved downhill in a fast, foaming torrent. She dived into it. The sound of water filled her ears, the rolling waves scared her. Her pursuers followed, headfirst. Rose began to spin, pulling the water towards her.

A wave swept her. She was now a few meters ahead of them. She prayed for another wave to come and convey her a little further. The dark-looking men were also playing their cards wisely. One of them dragged a thick log into the water, on which all the others fell and began to sail the current. They were now travelling at an improved speed. But Rose remained ahead. "Even if you swim like a fish, we must take you!" the tall one shouted.

A wind-driven wave from the north made it easier for her, it overturned the nautical log and the three men were toppled. They were all thrown deep into the water. Underneath, a clayish mud waited for their stubborn feet, which mired them down. It became impossible for them to escape this unplanned trap. Helpless, they floundered and made no more progress.

By now, Rose had almost reached land.

While on his way to the farm, Grandpa heard a crying voice.

"Is anyone there?"

"Come and help me!"

He stopped. "Where are you?"

The cry was coming from the other side of the river. Hurriedly he navigated the thick swamp which lay in front of him. From a distance he saw her green dress floating. She was holding onto a branch that was barely attached to a frail looking bamboo tree. In a split second, something horrible happened as he watched.

A fat crocodile jumped from the long grass on the right. The prey was well placed; the crocodile seemed excited. Rose seemed not to have noticed. "Crazzzzz!" the crocodile roared, but she was too focused on keeping her grip, fumes puffing up her nose.

"Rose!" Grandpa shouted at the top of his voice. She was up to her neck in the water, she was going to drop soon. "Don't give up, I'm coming to help!"

The crocodile drew nearer, opening its mouth, a mouth that seemed to contain all of eternity. Rose was indisputably in trouble. Grandpa attempted to reach towards her but fell instead into the river, his poor swimming skills almost making him drown. The already frantic Rose turned now but her eyes were not prepared for what they saw.

She was face-to-face with the crocodile. She froze, not knowing which direction to take. The choice was either to drown or be killed.

She made no choice.

Grandpa witnessed that choice-less moment. Rose was inches away from those murderous teeth when, in desperation, he threw a stick to deter the beast from its mission but it only opened its mouth wider. He witnessed this with his own eyes, screaming at the top of his voice with all the breath he had. But it was useless.

The mouth snapped shut, Rose had entered it for all eternity.

He met three men on his way back. Their clothes were soaking wet and they were blaming each other.

In the snap of a twig the news spread all over the village: their actions had been intended for a forceful marriage between Rose and the drunkard Jamalu, whose infamous proposal to each of his previous four wives had been "You either get married or die!"

As Grandpa ended his story my eyes were fixed on his elderly eyes, which were filled with sadness. I have never forgotten the look of grief and horror in his eyes.

A CHANCE ENCOUNTER WITH JACK BORMONT
Robert Ssempande

I arrived early at the Entebbe International Airport yesterday, ready to catch my flight to a new land: America. "I am heading home!" I kept telling myself. I had decided to leave for good.

The morning was sunny, but under that thick roof of the passenger terminal I barely noticed the heat. I sat there on a hard plastic bench in the lounge with my luggage right beside me, waiting for my flight. Quite a number of people were coming from the landing site.

An elderly Caucasian man dressed in blue jeans, red chequered shirt and a cowboy hat, came in first through the wide glass door, luggage in hand. He moved to the side as more people arrived and, for a moment, stood there. He glanced my way then started towards the lounge.

Other travellers were now swarming into the terminal. I was drawn to the intriguing gait of an extremely dark young man who entered, sporting a Drogba hairstyle. He passed by the benches with a swagger to his step as he spoke with one who seemed to be his brother.

"Look at your hair, only one weekend in Britain and you've become a *muyaye*? Humph!" his brother said.

"There's nothing at all wrong with this kind of hair, John," the young man replied, attempting to mimic a British accent.

As I sat there looking at these two, the elderly man came and set his luggage down against the bench.

"Hullo, son, how do you do?" He greeted, with a Texan accent, as he took off his hat.

"I am fine, *sir*," I replied, as it slowly dawned on me that the smile on his old face belonged to... *Hey, wait a second! I know this guy...* "Jack, I mean, Mr. Jack Bormont?" I said, astonished, as I rose from the bench.

"Yep, that's me," was his reply. "And you, sir?" He motioned with a tilt of his head.

"I am Ronald Blake." I replied, as we shook hands. "Wow, it's such an honour to meet you, sir. I'm a huge fan."

"Oh, really?" He raised his brow.

"Indeed, sir." *I mean, I grew up watching you on T.V as you inspired many in America, why wouldn't I be a fan?* "You, sir, are an inspiration to me, you and all that you stand for."

"Well, I'm pleased to hear that, but it's a greater honour for me to meet a lad like you who believes in our patriotic cause," he replied. "Mind if we sit down?"

"Not at all," I moved my luggage from the bench as I motioned him to sit where I had been seated.

"Why, thank ya, son." He said as he sat.

"So, what brings a man of your stature to a country like Uganda?" I asked.

"Oh, well, I'm just here to pay tribute to an old dear friend of mine."

"Oh, I see. An American in Uganda?"

"No, a Ugandan."

"A Ugandan?"

"Yep, but he's deceased."

"Sorry about that, sir, but it's a great surprise to find out that a man like you had a friend in Uganda."

"Ha-ha, you'd be amazed, son. Say, what kind of a last name is Blake?"

"Blake?"

"Yes, *Blake*, from what I learnt from my friend, last names are different here... It's not your custom now, is it?"

"Ah, no, not fully at least. But I decided to change my surname from the awful name Bulika to Blake, a radical step to your worldwide call, sir, embracing America as my new home."

"What!" He exclaimed, surprised. "Son, I never did tell anyone to leave their country and join mine."

"But I used to see you on TV, you kept saying your country is great. Well, isn't it?"

"Of course, it is, but you misunderstood me. I wasn't out to make folks abandon their homes and come to mine. I actually just wanted them to see the beauty of their own countries as I see the beauty of mine."

"But you spoke of America as though you wished us all to live there."

"No, no, I only spoke like that because I had so embraced my country with all her pros and cons, and I wanted everyone else

36

to do so for theirs."

"Okay, still, sir, America's cons are NOWHERE near Uganda's."

"So what? You jus' gon' cut yourself off from your own home and adopt a new one? If it's really as bad here as you say it is, then you gotta get this, son: it's not the fit soldier that needs savin', but the wounded one."

"How do you mean?"

"Lemme tell you a story. See, I was a soldier back home in the navy, back then in 1976. Well, like most folks, you may already know that. But what you might not know is that in those days we recruited many kinds of folks: African, Asian, Hispanics, you name 'em. But of these, there's only one I can never forget." He gestured with his index finger. "He was a Ugandan called Mukulo Mukisa. Well, that old doughboy was a soldier who fought not just for our country in the physical but for his own at heart; always dreamed about returnin' to his home after the war, but, well, me and the others always laughed it off; called it a fool's wish for anyone to want to leap back into Africa. Anyway, one night, the General comes and tells us we're goin' for a covert mission. And yeah, we went on the mission, but it went bad and I found myself maimed and alone behind enemy lines. My so-called buddies had written me off as a gone soldier, but Mukulo wouldn't let up; he sneaked right back into that jungle and came for me. 'In Uganda, a soldier is not a soldier but a brother, and I can never leave my brother behind,' he said as he carried me through that jungle, trailin' the others. I was struck by his solidarity with me, a man who had made fun of him and where he came from countless times. Just when we had caught up with the others, he was shot by an enemy spy that had been tracking us. We barely made it out, and without him..." He looked down. "We're all decorated with great honours back home, but not him, and yet he was the bravest of us all; still owe him ma darn life."

He paused for a moment with a wistful face, then straightened himself and continued.

"Son, there's two sides to the coin for any country. I've just given you the other for yours. See, you can do all kinds of things others have done, like that boy who was bouncin' like a carriage on a rough road ahead of me, but you will still be your country's child.

37

What you been tellin' me is that America ain't as much in need of savin' as your country is, and yet here you are, wantin' to leave. Well, the world would be no fun if we all were Americans, that's for sure. Look, the world needs Uganda's flavour, son; so, embrace it, like Mukulo embraced it. Embrace it, and then, see if you won't save this wounded soldier."

I KNOW WHO I AM
Gloria Kembabazi

"A man without identity does not belong," were the words I had heard. They had been said by the grey haired man with a wrinkled face who lived a few meters from home. I was trespassing on his patch of land, slinking past his straw thatched hut to the nearest shop.

I was clad in tight blue cotton shorts, a flaccid yellow blouse and blue slippers. His words struck like a spear in my chest. Yes, I was in the wrong but I needed to use the shortcut. A part of me was dribbling; it caused inordinate agony in my lower tummy.

I loathed strangers who felt they had a say in other people's lives. At times they chose words so carefully that, if you tried to ignore them, they would feast on your mind. I was once warned that people who had lived long were wise and that their words should never be ignored.

I was eight years old when I first encountered the old man. The garden behind his hut was my favourite hide-out while playing hide and seek. It was surrounded by gigantic yellow and green pumpkins and towering stalks of maize and sugarcane. You could take your time easing yourself there, unlike on the side of the road where you could be seen. I lowered my panties and eased myself.

I felt a tight grip on my arm as soon as I had finished. The shock was equivalent to that of electricity. His hand felt as rough as sandpaper. He let me go.

"*Kanawe, ronda eitaka oshweke ebiwakora!*" he ordered, instructing me to cover my mess with soil.

"*Tindabishweke,*" I objected. I could not understand why he wanted *me* to do it. Was it I who had to do the messy stuff?

"Do it yourself, after all it's your garden," I said, and ran.

The next thing I was conscious of was a man in a white robe standing next to my father, medicines in hand. Mother with sitting on my bed and bottles of Lucozade and Ribena stood on a stool invitingly. I smiled. I only had the chance to sip those when I was sick. Mother said I had missed a step and had had a terrible fall. I vowed never to cross the old man's path again.

Some years after that encounter I was doing my laundry when the gatekeeper approached me, looking startled.

"*Iwe, nomanya* , what's happened?" I signalled him to go on with a raise of my eyebrows.

"*Omuzeyi wa ahife yafa!*" The old man had passed away. I felt partially sorry, though since that fall I had attributed all my bad luck to him.

*

Garret, a big client who had given me my first break in PR, asked me out to a work related dinner. We met at Riaaz's Bistro, Nakasero. The restaurant was remarkably hushed. Like an eating exam, only fork, knife and plate utilized their ultimate right to make a sound. The waitress directed us to a free table. We ordered milkshakes; mint and vanilla.

"Tell me something new about you," Garret asked abruptly.

I could feel there was something specific he wanted me to talk about, although I could not figure it out.

"Well, I can't think of anything I haven't mentioned before."

"Uhm, okay. By the way, I checked out your writings."

"Oh great, thanks!"

"Sure. I wasn't amused much though."

That caught me by surprise. I was more used to the response that it was entertaining. The milkshakes arrived. I was frustrated by his words and shifted my attention to my drink. It had spume on top, typical of anything shaken.

"Damn! This milkshake looks so disgusting," I complained.

"You always make such bad choices," he mocked.

"So you weren't amused much? Tell me about it." Was he also not amused with the work I was doing for his company? Was the man I was grateful to for my job about to get me fired?

"Yeah sure," he said, staring into my eyes without affection. The same way he had at the interview when it did not cross my mind that he was noticing the colour of them. Was he noticing them now too? He still looked attractive even without affection. "Well, the thing is, young people are evading culture. You have a skill; nevertheless, you write about the wrong stuff." He sipped his drink as if trying to swallow the awkwardness that had come with his statement.

"It depends on what you mean by *wrong stuff*," I defended. "Don't all bloggers write about their observations, thoughts, things that appeal to them?" I managed to say with a puckered brow.

"True, but if you wrote about things that appeal to your culture as well, that would help pass it on rather than taking on the American liberal way of doing things. You must know Byamugisha of New Vision, an incredibly great writer. Writing about his culture has made him so famous and rich."

"In other words, it is because of fame and money that you criticise my not writing about my culture?"

"No, not precisely, it's about what defines you. Your identity, who you are and where you belong, and a man without identity does not belong."

I looked at Garret warily for any clues of his body being inhabited by a ghost. The words of the old man had been exactly the same.

Had the old man meant that I had no respect for my culture? Was it the skimpy garments and sharp pointing stilettos that I always donned? Or my lack of mannerisms, not saying 'hello' to everyone I met on the road? Was I to blame or was it society?

"Aren't we are all shaped by society? Aren't the differences between our values and norms present because you were brought up in a conservative community while I was raised in a liberal one?" I asked rhetorically.

"But that should not be an excuse not to know who you are," he insisted, leaning back in his seat with a wry smile.

I nodded in disbelief. 'Just because I do not wear a t-shirt with the words *I love my culture* scribbled on it, that doesn't imply otherwise,' I assured him. 'People are individually defined by their inner self and what they love to do, isn't that so?'

He was silent.

'I know who I am and I belong!' I said, looking him straight in the eye with my voice raised brusquely at him, but directing the words to the old man.

STOLEN INNOCENCE
Nadweny Faith Naome

I have had all but a century's existence on Earth, lived a life buoyed by pride and characterised by surrender to fate's whims. My envious surrogate of a mother, who only saw me as a sentimental object, tried failingly to break my spirit but I am stronger than that, true to her word my real mother watches over me as she promised.

It was on 14th October 1972 that I found the true nature of Celine, my adoptive mother, and how deep her hatred for me ran. That evening, for no particular reason I can spell, I was abnormally happy on my way from the garden. All of a sudden a large man, with skin as black as coal, teeth stained from chewing tobacco leaves, a balding head and large round eyes stepped out from the secluded bushes by the dusty roadside on the way home. Shirt askew and pantaloons that didn't fit quite well, he made a faint attempt to smile; a menacing smile it was. My nostrils twitched in protest when the pungent smell of liquor coming off him hit me in the face. The warning in my head echoed the terror in my heart but setting that aside, I managed a calm greeting.

He leered at me, his hungry eyes searched every part of my body.

He licked his lips and said in a thick rapid accent "You shud-obey-yowa-elders-unquestioningly."

He smacked his lips together as if in preparation to devour a bountiful meal. He made a grab for me and I ducked out of his reach then tripped all over my feet.

He laughed that half crazed laugh and mumbled, "De mo' yuh try ta run, de rougha I will mek it for yuh. I 'av ta get my money. Promith ta mek it swift and it'll be oba before yuh knew it."

As he drew nearer, fear held me in its thrall. I wanted to shout, I wanted to call out for help but I was numb with shock.

"Yowa Celine told I ta got my money's worth," he said. I thought of my step mother. Did she really hate me that much?

I silently muttered *Mama , watch over your little girl* as I made frantic attempts to fight him off. I tried to scream and he choked down my breath with his palm. From within the urge to fight rose, as fierce as a lion's roar, and my teeth sank down hard into his heavy hand. When his screech of agony pierced the night I pried free of his grip and connected my knee to his groin. He doubled over in pain and I took off as fast as my legs could carry me.

I made it home in one piece. That memory had forever seared itself on my mind and left me a trembling mass of nerves. I cried my heart out knowing that, however much I wanted the whole world to know the devil I had for a step mother, it was my word against that of the so-called respected elder. Besides, I also feared condemning myself to a life of discrimination and segregation that was at the time characteristic of young girls who accused their elders of scheming against them. The truth has a funny way of tainting people's innocence and preying upon their pride to disgrace them.

"You had better surface from wherever you are hiding, you ungrateful louse!" Stepmother's shout took me out of my reverie. I had been seated by the *Nyambalabutonya* tree, probably because I identified with its stature surviving all conditions, as must I survive my life born into servitude.

I am Muryagyi Jacinta, infamously known as Muryagyi of the sombre smile, for it is said that there was something about me that struck a chord in almost everybody's heart. I high-tailed it out of my hideout, lest she thought up more ways of punishing me for being tardy. My welcome was, as usual, slaps from softened hands to my already abused body and battered spirit.

She jeered at me and my mother silently rebelled, *"Yes! She is jealous of you - of the grace in your walk, the perseverance from within and the beauty inherent."*

Celine and her above reproach daughters could never be content of their appearances for as long as I was nearby. Suzanna and Sarah were the laziest girls whose work was to act lofty and talk about time-wasting topics. She always beamed when talking about her son, the major accomplishment in her life. A slap landed on my cheek to accompany her order that I fetch firewood and do all the other chores, while her daughters only waited for meal time in order to satisfy their healthy appetites.

I was born to Kankane Patrick, a man to whom nothing else mattered but his position as Village Chief. His one life's goal was making as many embittered enemies as the sands of the beach and in this he was as successful as the sunrise each morning. He taught his son to be silently commanding around the eyes so as to follow in his footsteps.

I was the outcast, the one child of all that bore little resemblance to him but for the eyes I possessed. I was the spitting image of my Munyankole mother. I was an addition to his swiftly rising number of children from different mothers yet the least wanted. Is there any justice in not being wanted by your own flesh and blood?

It now seems that Celine had his blessings to turn me into a slave because he never seemed to mind at all. For each tear I shed for the awakening kicks at 4:00 am and the times I was chased from the dining table, with an excuse as falsely feeble as not having washed my hands, or the animosity directed at me for suggesting that I start school, he seemed blinded by the worm that is love yet it appeared to be witchcraft in my eyes. To my father I was a misbegotten memory, thus he was dead to my heart and his name ceased to cross my lips.

His societal position made him popular and Celine only rejoiced in her new found graces, for she had been but a farmer's daughter before he took any interest in her. She enjoyed playing hostess and found great pleasure in parading me around in decently styled clothes for the benefit of the guests, symbolizing that I was a big part of the family, an accepted member of her "loving" family. In the presence of all those guests the show extended to a hug, as she did with her own daughters, and threatened violence if I didn't smile that captivating smile to reassure everyone that she was a kind and caring mother.

In the dark evenings, in my usual resting place near the fireplace with mosquitoes for companions, I wished for death to carry me to my late mother's embrace but all I heard was the echo of her tearful voice telling me to hold fast to my dreams, to never forget that there is sunshine after rain.

Before the restless sleep that always claimed my exhausted body took control I only wished for whatever was done to me in the darkness, and behind closed doors, to one day come out into the light. After all, a leopard doesn't change its spots, and neither did Celine.

44

TRUE TO NOTHING
Mildred Apenyo

Half of Atim's body is already out of the taxi when she snags her sandal on a piece of metal jutting out of its floor. She throws her hands out for balance, or for luck, and yelps as her foot meets the dusty ground.

It takes a while for her eyes to adjust to the white glare of the petrol station's fluorescent bulbs, but this doesn't stop her from moving. She would rather sprain her ankle while stumbling to safety than risk being swept off the murram by an impatient driver.

Satisfied that she's reached a spot where no vehicle will take her bones by surprise, Atim turns towards the shed where boda boda cyclists usually congregate. She's chewing on the inside of her cheek in a way that gives her mouth a pouty, lopsided look and for a minute her eyes remain fixed on the chipping varnish of her toenails.

Atim jerks her head up and stares into the shed. It's empty. She jeers long and loud, even though she didn't expect any rider to be there. They've taken to leaving for home earlier and earlier, as if boda work is just a pastime for them.

She considers hailing one of the random cyclists zipping past. Considers it only briefly. Not much time has passed since the incident with the running men:

Two men had run past her and Kakuru - her regular bodaman - shouting that there were thieves on the road ahead. Kakuru had slowed the motorcycle down and hesitated at the mouth of the route that led to Atim's home. She was terrified and had decided to make him ride back, to the main road, when he had revved the engine and torn down the road they had just been warned against. Trust is essential between oneself and one's bodaman. Trust was all that had quelled the fit of suspicion that had made Atim consider plunging a Bic pen into Kakuru's neck.

So even after three motorcycles have circled her, with their riders assuring her of how well they know "*ewa Mzee,*" she waits for a familiar face; or tries to. The third man senses her desperation and remains within earshot, calling out details that are supposed to convince her that he's the man for the job.

"Your Mzee know me from stage up there."

"You buy breakfast from my business at stage sometimes!"

"I take your sister and brother to Nakasero Primary!"

The kids haven't studied at Nakasero for a year now, but Atim glances at her watch and decides that, if he's a thief, he's done his research and deserves some sort of chance. She runs over, pulls the back of her skirt between her legs, and straddles the motorcycle.

The man doesn't stop trying to impress her with the scope of his knowledge about her family, not even when they're moving. "I know everyone in dat home. Your father, your mother, only your mother she get lost," he says.

That's one way to put it, alright. She got lost.

"You come home very late from work..."

Atim's eyes narrow. Heavy words gather on her tongue like rain clouds.

"So, why do you come late? Is there a problem you have?"

Irritation spreads across her mind like goose pimples. He wouldn't be asking such questions if it were her 17 year old brother on the motorcycle. She doesn't answer, instead concentrating on the line of ragged plants that frame the road.

After a short silence he says, "I'm not see her, your mother, for long, by the way. Is she the one who died last year here? I know somebody died around here because that was the time my wife got pregnant."

Atim isn't prepared for the indignation that slams into her chest and she shifts roughly, making the motorcycle veer towards a small tree. She is flattened by how casually he marks the death of her mother with the occasion of his own slime finding a home in some womb.

Her resolve to remain calm blows straight out of her ears and into the wind. She tells him, "Shut up! Do your job!" Finding herself unable to remain so close to him she orders him to kill the engine. She slaps two thousand shillings on the seat of the motorcycle and stomps away.

Who knows, this idiot might deliver me head first into a wall and mark my death with some other event related to his loins.

Atim takes one, two, three deep breaths and tries to forget her irritation, but it is stubborn and refuses to fade. It's starting to fray, that frame of mind that she's been constructing all day to help her survive the next minutes of emotional diarrhoea. It's starting to split like the inner seams of a too tight pair of jeans.

As always when she hasn't spent the night at home, in the house, with her remaining people, Atim has to fight through tangles of guilt. She can never shake the feeling that she's betraying her mother and the baby. *The baby. My baby? Mum's baby?*

The diarrhoea notices a weak point and licks at it, eventually bursting through and completely covering her mind. Atim's mind becomes a blur of voices, a podium that all her anxieties gleefully clamber onto and mock her from.

The red gate to her father's home is within sight now, every step she makes is tortured. She pulls her phone out and is about to dial the maid's number when she notices a message from Michael: "Think about it."

Atim leans against the gate and weeps until she starts to feel foolish, like a person pretending to be in a movie. Their last moments tonight had been awkward. It's not that she wasn't into it, into him. The burden of *lateness* had tainted everything. Michael had been moving on top of her for so long that she'd begun to resent him and was about to push him off when he gasped, started to thrust faster, and contorted his face into that series of expressions that always made her laugh.

Michael has been talking about that yawning expanse called "the future" a lot lately. Atim finds herself unable to articulate the kaleidoscope of feelings that flood her whenever he begs for her to move into the tiny apartment he shares with his cousin. She's terrified he'll stop asking. She's irritated when he does.

She dials the maid's number. "Christine! Yab dogola!" The maid arrives quickly, too quickly, which annoys Atim. She was hoping to gain ground, make the woman timid by snapping about sluggishness. The maid looks her up and down and says, "Oh. So you're back?" Atim makes a show of slamming the door when she enters the house.

I hope dad is asleep.

The living room is messy. A bowl of congealed porridge sits abandoned on a sofa, newspapers carpet the floor. The house seems dead. Atim imagines, for a terrible moment, that the maid has poisoned everyone, until she hears squeals coming from the direction of the baby's room.

Can this kid smell me?

She kicks off her shoes and walks towards the noise. Wrinkling her nose at the oversweet smell of milk and powder, she scoops the chubby child into her arms and wiggles her eyebrows. A stream of giggles tumbles out of his mouth.

Atim settles carefully on a loveseat and bounces him on her lap, giggling back at him with an excitement that grows and grows until it's real.

OF LOVE AND SISYPHEAN TASKS
Kirabo Nora

"I'm good at forgetting," I said, my voice shaking, pleading for him. I finally had him but my mind was racing, sense and reason were losing out to my feelings for James.

"This is too good to be true. It will come crushing down... on you!" My inner voice screamed, but I buried the doubt with the memory of all my failed romances.

He was here but not really here. I reached out to caress his beard. I hated his beard, but I had long suffered it in silence for the sake of those stolen kisses. He pulled my hand deliberately away from his face, ever the self-conscious one.

"Well I'm not good at forgetting. How can I forget her?" he said.

Her.

I wondered why I could not rid myself of love triangles, in my relationships there was always me, him and a "her". Why should this be different? It was the equivalent of an intro to a bad porno, and indeed it evoked the same disgust.

I snatched my hand from his. "Before, we were wrong because she was in the way, so to speak," I took two steps away from him, now letting my voice rise without restraint. I was retreating like a wounded lioness, a thing I had failed to be for too long. I wanted to lunge at him, fangs out, to rip his neck from his shoulders... but I loved that head.

"Now..." I paused when I realised I was screaming like the old woman who sold avocadoes at the corner of my apartment block. I took a deep breath to calm myself. "Now it's because she's ... not in the way?"

My voice trailed to a whisper to understand this cruel twist of fate.

"Who are you?" the plump receptionist asked me. Her voice broke me out of the trance, the memory still fresh from three weeks ago. I had stomped out of the room. Now I was here. I altered my gaze to meet hers.

So who am I?

I dread this question. Am I just a name, a gender, or a representative of an age group? By providing these statistics would this secretary really know who I was?

Before I could answer her invasive question, her phone rang. It was a wonder how fast she was distracted from her exploratory mission. Now she completely forgot about me as she spoke in hushed tones and with an occasional giggle. Maybe it was her lover. I used to giggle like that when James called. I drowned her out to sink into the deep waters of my mind.

Every time I had thought of him with her I had been overcome with jealousy. I mused at how she must have felt when she suspected that there was another woman. How she must have laid her head on the pillow awaiting his calls, unaware that his hands were busy. And the next day he would rob her of her fears with deceit, claiming he was overcome with sleep. Perhaps what he meant to say was he was overcome with lust.

I always imagined him holding her body in a protective yet hungry way. He never held me like that. Still, the way he held me had made my heart skip once too often. Even after she was gone she was still his, and he was still hers. This was my mantra. When his hand caressed my thigh it was her hand on him that he thought of. I had to come to terms with the fact that, although it seemed like I could have him, I would never really have him. I had distanced myself from those soul-sucking pleasures.

And yet, here I was, again! I must finally exorcise that demon. Only then will I find normalcy in being away from him. Only then will I crave others like I used to, before him.

I always wondered how he could sleep amidst my loud snores. Why wasn't he repulsed by that side to me? But then I remembered that human beings could go to unimaginable lengths for love and even greater ones to satisfy the flesh's hunger. It was the latter. I know he rode the waves of sleep unaware of the snores.

At dawn I would let him have his way with me. He would immerse himself into this trifling encounter and after he had tired himself out he would escape my wondering gaze. He knew that within my eyes lay my desire to be wanted, to be loved. He would flee these cries and I was left with myself. I would stare at myself in the mirror and fail to recognise her in me. I was to spend eternity with a woman I did not know.

"Excuse me, nyabo?" she said after putting down her phone.

Her voice seemed to claw through my thoughts to forcefully wrench me from the depths of my memory. I turned back to face her but her eyes were stuck on the scar above my eyebrow. The scar I had received when I was 13 years old from going up a tree with my brother. I had always been a follower, but somewhere down the road I always forgot the rules that came with that title. I forgot to look out for myself. The reminder was this scar; the sole etch on my brown face. The same scar that James would stroke gently as he held me, saying: "It is a reminder that you are the stronger one, how else could you put up with a bastard like me?" He would say it as joke, but we both knew it was true.

I followed her gaze that now took in my small frame, as she rolled her eyes. Was that jealousy I detected? It was as if by determining whether my hair was real she would have somehow solved the mystery at hand.

"My name?" I blurted out, trying to remember my purpose. The realisation that I was here to find freedom only served to unnerve me. "It's Evelyn. Evelyn Kobusingye," I said, summoning my inner James Bond in an attempt to hide the fear in my voice.

"Do you have an appointment madam?" the secretary asked. I could almost taste the irritation seeping from her venomous mouth, a mouth that had undoubtedly invoked fear in others like me.

"No, I do not have one. But Mr. Mabugo James must be expecting me."

She responded with a knowing look.

Maybe there really were others I thought to myself, as I took the seat. But it didn't matter because every bit of my being knew that this was the end. James was predictable. Our next conversation would go like the rest. *I am sorry for hurting you, I will change*. He would say this after dinner. He wouldn't take any calls. He would look me in my eyes and kiss me softly. Then he would be James again.

I was once again brought back to reality by the sound of the secretary.

"Nyabo?" she called out, as though she had spent the past hour hounding me for my name. "Mr. Mabugo will see you now," she

51

said, rolling her eyes. I insisted on my defiant smile as I slowly stood up. The last time I had seen him I had stormed off, the typical scene for our break-ups.

This time it felt different. This time there would be no more James.

Acknowledgements

It is said that it takes a village to raise a child. Indeed, it took a community to bring forth this anthology. The anthology is a key component of the Writivism program of the Centre for African Cultural Excellence.

The program commenced in October 2012. with a call for entries of short fiction on the themes of Identity, Diversity and Equality from emerging writers aged fifteen to twenty five years of age. Forty three entries were received and twenty three writers selected by a panel comprising Hilda Twongyeirwe and Beatrice Lamwaka of Uganda Association of Women Writers (FEMRITE), Harriet Anena of The Monitor Publications, Ernest Bazanye of Uganda Modern Literary Digest, Novuyo Rosa Tshuma (then of Centre for African Cultural Excellence) and Ceris Dien of Kushinda.

Nineteen of these writers attended a one-day Creative Writing workshop in January 2013 facilitated by writers Zukiswa Wanner, Okwiri Oduor, Beatrice Lamwaka and Constance Obonyo. The nineteen were assigned mentors who guided them to develop their stories further. The mentors included Olisakwe Ukamaka, Emmanuel Iduma, Richard Ali, Beatrice Lamwaka, Dami Ajayi, Novuyo Rosa Tshuma and Abubakar Adam Ibrahim.

Fourteen stories were longlisted, following the mentoring. They were published at Readers Cafe Africa and Short Story Day Africa websites and The Observer (Uganda) newspaper. The fourteen writers toured seven schools around Kampala, where they discussed their stories with students.

A three-member panel comprising Zukiswa Wanner (Chair), Ayodelle Morroco-Clarke and Ernest Bazanye shortlisted five stories which were then published in The Munyori Literary Journal, on The Monitor newspaper website and at www.writivism.wordpress.com, for public voting. The shortlisted writers held public readings at the FEMRITE Readers Club, Open Mic Uganda and The Lantern Meet of Poets, where audiences also selected their favourite stories. The longlisted writers also voted for their favourite stories, from the short-listed five.

A winner and two Runners-up were announced at the Writivism mini-Festival in Kampala. This anthology, jointly published by Kushinda and Boda Books (the Centre for African

Cultural Excellence's publishing imprint) comprises all the fourteen longlisted stories.

The 2012/3 Writivism program was in a piloting stage, and was generously funded by The British Council Global Changemakers program and the Open Society Initiative for Eastern Africa. The project also benefited from a lot of in-kind contributions and donations from individuals and organisations. We are eternally grateful for all the support and goodwill extended to this project. We look forward to brighter years ahead.

Brian Bwesigye
Co-Founder, Centre for African Cultural Excellence

December 2013

Kampala, Uganda

Writivism 2014 Short Story Prize Submission Guidelines

Opening date – 8 February 2014

Closing date - 30th April 2014

Entries must be submitted online, on the Writivism website. No mark as to the identity of the writer should be made on the story itself. No entries will be considered if submitted after this date. The competition long-list (of fifteen stories) shall be announced on the 15th of May 2014 and the short-list (of five stories) on the 1st of June 2014. Winners shall be announced on Short Story Day Africa, the 21st of June 2014 at an Awards Evening during the Writivism Mini-Festival 2014 in Kampala, Uganda.

1. The Writivism Short Story Prize is an annual award for emerging African writers administered by the Center for African Cultural Excellence (CACE).

2. Entrants must be unpublished writers, resident in an African country. One is deemed published if they have a book of their own. Self-published books do not count.

3. There will be five sub-regional winners (Eastern, Western, Central, Southern and Northern) and one overall winner. The overall winner of the Writivism Short Story Prize will receive UGX 1,000,000, second place winner UGX 500,000, third place winner UGX 250,000 and the remaining five regional winners UGX 200,000.

4. Questions of eligibility shall be resolved by the CACE administration and their decision is final.

5. Entries must be submitted online, by uploading them on the Writivism website.

6. Only one entry per writer may be submitted for the Writivism Short Story Prize. The story must be original and previously unpublished in any form except on the writer's personal blog.

7. All entries must be in English, and 2,000 - 3,000 words long.

8. Entries should be attached in Microsoft Word or Rich Text formats, with the title of the story as the file name. The first page of the story should include the name of the story and the number of words. The entry must be typed in Times New Roman 12 point font and 1.5 line spacing. No mention should be made on the identity of the writer in the entry.

9. Entrants agree as a condition of entry that CACE may publicize the fact that a story has been entered, longlisted or shortlisted for the Prize. The shortlisted writers and winners of the competition will be expected to participate in readings, The Writivism mini-Festival and school tours.

10. Worldwide copyright of each story remains with the writer. CACE will have the unrestricted right to publish the long-listed stories in an anthology and for promotional purposes.

11. Prize sub-regions; *Eastern Africa* (Uganda, Rwanda, Burundi, Tanzania, Kenya, South Sudan, Somalia, Djibouti, Ethiopia and Eritrea);*Central Africa* (Angola, Democratic Republic of Congo, Central African Republic, Congo Brazaville, Chad, Gabon, Equatorial Guinea, Sao Tome and Principe, Cameroon and Niger); *Northern Africa* (Egypt, Mali, Mauritania, Western Sahara, Morocco, Algeria, Libya, Tunisia and Sudan); *Southern Africa* (South Africa, Mozambique, Zimbabwe, Namibia, Zambia, Malawi, Botswana, Madagascar, Lesotho and Swaziland) *and Western Africa* (Nigeria, Benin, Togo, Ghana, Ivory Coast, Liberia, Sierra Leone, Guinea Conakry, Guinea Bissau, Gambia and Senegal).